MW00623242

LEAF BY NIGGLE

LEAF BY NIGGLE

J.R.R. Tolkien.

HarperCollins*Publishers*

HarperCollins*Publishers*
1 London Bridge Street,
London SE1 9GF
www.tokien.co.uk

This paperback edition 2016
13

'Leaf by Niggle' first published in *Tree and Leaf*
copyright © The Tolkien Trust 1964

Afterword excerpted from *Tales from the Perilous Realm*
copyright © Tom Shippey 2008

® and Tolkien® are registered trade marks of
The Tolkien Estate Limited

ISBN 978-0-00-820553-9

Set in Stempel Garamond

Printed and bound in Great Britain by
CPI Group (UK) Ltd, Croydon CR0 4YY

All rights reserved. No part of this publication may be
reproduced, stored in a retrieval system, or transmitted, in any
form or by any means, electronic, mechanical, photocopying,
recording or otherwise, without the prior permission of
the publishers.

MIX
Paper from
responsible sources
FSC® C007454

This book is sold subject to the condition that it shall not, by way of trade
or otherwise, be lent, re-sold, hired out or otherwise circulated without the
publishers' prior consent in any form of binding or cover other than that
in which it is published and without a similar condition including
this condition being imposed on the subsequent purchaser.

Find out more about HarperCollins and the environment at
www.harpercollins.co.uk/green

LEAF BY NIGGLE

BY

J.R.R. Tolkien

'THIS STORY was not published until 1947 (in *Dublin Review*). It has not been changed since it reached manuscript form, very swiftly, one day when I awoke with it already in mind. One of its sources was a great-limbed poplar tree that I could see even lying in bed. It was suddenly lopped and mutilated by its owner, I do not know why. It is cut down now, a less barbarous punishment for any crimes it may have been accused of, such as being large and alive. I do not think it had any friends, or any mourners, except myself and a pair of owls.'

J.R.R. Tolkien[1]

---

[1] From the 'Introductory Note' to *Tree and Leaf*, 1964.

THERE WAS ONCE a little man called Niggle, who had a long journey to make. He did not want to go, indeed the whole idea was distasteful to him; but he could not get out of it. He knew he would have to start sometime, but he did not hurry with his preparations.

Niggle was a painter. Not a very successful one, partly because he had many other things to do. Most of these things he thought were a nuisance; but he did them fairly well, when he could not get out of them: which (in his opinion) was far too often. The laws in his country were rather strict. There were other hindrances, too. For one thing, he was sometimes just idle, and did nothing at all. For another, he was kindhearted, in a way. You know the sort of kind heart: it made him uncomfortable more often than it made him do anything; and even when he did anything, it did not prevent him from grumbling, losing his temper and swearing (mostly to himself). All the same, it did land him in a good many odd jobs for his neighbour, Mr Parish, a man with a lame leg. Occasionally he even helped other people from further off, if they came and asked him to. Also, now and again, he remembered his journey, and began to pack a few things in an ineffectual way: at such times he did not paint very much.

He had a number of pictures on hand; most of them were too large and ambitious for his skill. He was the sort of painter who can paint leaves better than trees. He used to spend a long time on a single leaf, trying to catch its shape, and its sheen, and the glistening of dewdrops on its edges. Yet he wanted to paint a whole tree, with all of its leaves in the same style, and all of them different.

There was one picture in particular which bothered him. It had begun with a leaf caught in the wind, and it became a tree; and the tree grew, sending out innumerable branches, and thrusting out the most fantastic roots. Strange birds came and settled on the twigs and had to be attended to. Then all round the Tree, and behind it, through the gaps in the leaves and boughs, a country began to open out; and there were glimpses of a forest marching over the land, and of mountains tipped with snow. Niggle lost interest in his other pictures; or else he took them and tacked them on to the edges of his great picture. Soon the canvas became so large that he had to get a ladder, and he ran up and down it, putting in a touch here, and rubbing out a patch there. When people came to call, he seemed polite enough, though he fiddled a little with the pencils on his desk. He listened to what they said, but underneath he was thinking all the time about his big canvas, in the tall shed that had been built for it out in his garden (on a plot where once he had grown potatoes).

He could not get rid of his kind heart. 'I wish I was more strong-minded' he sometimes said to himself, meaning that he wished other people's troubles did not make him feel uncomfortable. But for a long time he was not seriously perturbed. 'At any rate, I shall get this one picture done, my real picture, before I have to go on that wretched journey,' he used to say. Yet he was beginning to see that he could not put off his start indefinitely. The picture would have to stop just growing and get finished.

One day, Niggle stood a little way off from his picture and considered it with unusual attention and detachment. He could not make up his mind what he thought about it, and wished he had some friend who would tell him what to think. Actually it seemed to him wholly unsatisfactory, and yet very lovely, the only really beautiful picture in the world. What he would have liked at that moment would have been to see himself walk in, and slap him on the back and say (with obvious sincerity): 'Absolutely magnificent! I see exactly what you are getting at. Do get on with it, and don't bother about anything else! We will arrange for a public pension, so that you need not.'

However, there was no public pension. And one thing he could see: it would need some concentration, some *work*, hard uninterrupted work, to finish the picture, even at its present size. He rolled up his sleeves, and began to concentrate. He tried for several days not to bother about other things. But there came a tremendous crop of interruptions. Things went wrong in his house; he had to go and serve on a jury in the town; a distant friend fell ill; Mr Parish was laid up with lumbago; and visitors kept on coming. It was springtime, and they wanted a free tea in the country: Niggle lived in a pleasant little house, miles away from the town. He cursed them in his heart, but he could not deny that he had invited them himself, away back in the winter, when he had not thought it an 'interruption' to visit the shops and have tea with acquaintances in the town. He tried to harden his heart; but it was not a success. There were many things that he had not the face to say *no* to, whether he thought them duties or not; and there were some things he was compelled to do, whatever he thought. Some of his visitors hinted that his garden was rather neglected, and that he might get a visit from an Inspector. Very few of them knew about his picture, of course; but if they had known, it would not have made much difference. I doubt if they would have thought that it mattered much. I dare say it was not really a very good picture, though it may have had some good passages. The Tree, at any rate, was curious. Quite unique in its way. So was Niggle; though he was also a very ordinary and rather silly little man.

At length Niggle's time became really precious. His acquaintances in the distant town began to remember that the little man had got to make a troublesome journey, and some began to calculate how long at the latest he could put off starting. They wondered who would take his house, and if the garden would be better kept.

The autumn came, very wet and windy. The little painter was in his shed. He was up on the ladder, trying to catch the gleam of the westering sun on the peak of a snow-mountain, which he had glimpsed just to the left of the leafy tip of one of the Tree's branches. He knew that he would have to be leaving soon: perhaps early next year. He could only just get the picture finished, and only so so, at that: there were some corners where he would not have time now to do more than hint at what he wanted.

There was a knock on the door. 'Come in!' he said sharply, and climbed down the ladder. He stood on the floor twiddling his brush. It was his neighbour, Parish: his only real neighbour, all other folk lived a long way off. Still, he did not like the man very much: partly because he was so often in trouble and in need of help; and also because he did not care about painting, but was very critical about gardening. When Parish looked at Niggle's garden (which was often) he saw mostly weeds; and when he looked at Niggle's pictures (which was seldom) he saw only green and grey patches and black lines, which seemed to him nonsensical. He did not mind mentioning the weeds (a neighbourly duty), but he refrained from giving any opinion of the pictures. He thought this was very kind, and he did not realise that, even if it was kind, it was not kind enough. Help with the weeds (and perhaps praise for the pictures) would have been better.

'Well, Parish, what is it?' said Niggle.

'I oughtn't to interrupt you, I know,' said Parish (without a glance at the picture). 'You are very busy, I'm sure.'

Niggle had meant to say something like that himself, but he had missed his chance. All he said was: 'Yes.'

'But I have no one else to turn to,' said Parish.

'Quite so,' said Niggle with a sigh: one of those sighs that are a private comment, but which are not made quite inaudible. 'What can I do for you?'

'My wife has been ill for some days, and I am getting worried,' said Parish. 'And the wind has blown half the tiles off my roof, and water is pouring into the bedroom. I think I ought to get the doctor. And the builders, too, only they take so long to come. I was wondering if you had any wood and canvas you could spare, just to patch me up and see me through for a day or two.' Now he did look at the picture.

'Dear, dear!' said Niggle. 'You *are* unlucky. I hope it is no more than a cold that your wife has got. I'll come round presently, and help you move the patient downstairs.'

'Thank you very much,' said Parish, rather coolly. 'But it is not a cold, it is a fever. I should not have bothered you for a cold. And my wife is in bed downstairs already. I can't get up and down with trays, not with my leg. But I see you are busy. Sorry to have troubled you. I had rather hoped you might have been able to spare the time to go for the doctor, seeing how I'm placed; and the builder too, if you really have no canvas you can spare.'

'Of course,' said Niggle; though other words were in his heart, which at the moment was merely soft without feeling at all kind. 'I could go. I'll go, if you are really worried.'

'I am worried, very worried. I wish I was not lame,' said Parish.

So Niggle went. You see, it was awkward. Parish was his neighbour, and everyone else a long way off. Niggle had a bicycle, and Parish had not, and could not ride one. Parish had a lame leg, a genuine lame leg which gave him a good deal of pain: that had to be remembered, as well as his sour expression and whining voice. Of course, Niggle had a picture and barely time to finish it. But it seemed that this was a thing that Parish had to reckon with and not Niggle. Parish, however, did not reckon with pictures; and Niggle could not alter that. 'Curse it!' he said to himself, as he got out his bicycle.

It was wet and windy, and daylight was waning. 'No more work for me today!' thought Niggle, and all the time that he was riding, he was either swearing to himself, or imagining the strokes of his brush on the mountain, and on the spray of leaves beside it, that he had first imagined in the spring. His fingers twitched on the handlebars. Now he was out of the shed, he saw exactly the way in which to treat that shining spray which framed the distant vision of the mountain. But he had a sinking feeling in his heart, a sort of fear that he would never now get a chance to try it out.

Niggle found the doctor, and he left a note at the builder's. The office was shut, and the builder had gone home to his fireside. Niggle got soaked to the skin, and caught a chill himself. The doctor did not set out as promptly as Niggle had done. He arrived next day, which was quite convenient for him, as by that time there were two patients to deal with, in neighbouring houses. Niggle was in bed, with a high temperature, and marvellous patterns of leaves and involved branches forming in his head and on the ceiling. It did not comfort him to learn that Mrs Parish had only had a cold, and was getting up. He turned his face to the wall and buried himself in leaves.

He remained in bed some time. The wind went on blowing. It took away a good many more of Parish's tiles, and some of Niggle's as well: his own roof began to leak. The builder did not come. Niggle did not care; not for a day or two. Then he crawled out to look for some food (Niggle had no wife). Parish did not come round: the rain had got into his leg and made it ache; and his wife was busy mopping up water, and wondering if 'that Mr Niggle' had forgotten to call at the builder's. Had she seen any chance of borrowing anything useful, she would have sent Parish round, leg or no leg; but she did not, so Niggle was left to himself.

At the end of a week or so Niggle tottered out to his shed again. He tried to climb the ladder, but it made his head giddy. He sat and looked at the picture, but there were no patterns of leaves or visions of mountains in his mind that day. He could have painted a far-off view of a sandy desert, but he had not the energy.

Next day he felt a good deal better. He climbed the ladder, and began to paint. He had just begun to get into it again, when there came a knock on the door.

'Damn!' said Niggle. But he might just as well have said 'Come in!' politely, for the door opened all the same. This time a very tall man came in, a total stranger.

'This is a private studio,' said Niggle. 'I am busy. Go away!'

'I am an Inspector of Houses,' said the man, holding up his appointment-card, so that Niggle on his ladder could see it.

'Oh!' he said.

'Your neighbour's house is not satisfactory at all,' said the Inspector.

'I know,' said Niggle. 'I took a note to the builder's a long time ago, but they have never come. Then I have been ill.'

'I see,' said the Inspector. 'But you are not ill now.'

'But I'm not a builder. Parish ought to make a

complaint to the Town Council, and get help from the Emergency Service.'

'They are busy with worse damage than any up here,' said the Inspector. 'There has been a flood in the valley, and many families are homeless. You should have helped your neighbour to make temporary repairs and prevent the damage from getting more costly to mend than necessary. That is the law. There is plenty of material here: canvas, wood, waterproof paint.'

'Where?' asked Niggle indignantly.

'There!' said the Inspector, pointing to the picture.

'My picture!' exclaimed Niggle.

'I dare say it is,' said the Inspector. 'But houses come first. That is the law.'

'But I can't . . .' Niggle said no more, for at that moment another man came in. Very much like the Inspector he was, almost his double: tall, dressed all in black.

'Come along!' he said. 'I am the Driver.'

Niggle stumbled down from the ladder. His fever seemed to have come on again, and his head was swimming; he felt cold all over.

'Driver? Driver?' he chattered. 'Driver of what?'

'You, and your carriage,' said the man. 'The

carriage was ordered long ago. It has come at last. It's waiting. You start today on your journey, you know.'

There now!' said the Inspector. 'You'll have to go; but it's a bad way to start on your journey, leaving your jobs undone. Still, we can at least make some use of this canvas now.'

'Oh dear!' said poor Niggle, beginning to weep. 'And it's not even finished!'

'Not finished!' said the Driver. 'Well, it's finished with, as far as you're concerned, at any rate. Come along!'

Niggle went, quite quietly. The Driver gave him no time to pack, saying that he ought to have done that before, and they would miss the train; so all Niggle could do was to grab a little bag in the hall. He found that it contained only a paint-box and a small book of his own sketches: neither food nor clothes. They caught the train all right. Niggle was feeling very tired and sleepy; he was hardly aware of what was going on when they bundled him into his compartment. He did not care much: he had forgotten where he was supposed to be going, or what he was going for. The train ran almost at once into a dark tunnel.

Niggle woke up in a very large, dim railway station. A Porter went along the platform shouting, but he was not shouting the name of the place; he was shouting *Niggle!*

Niggle got out in a hurry, and found that he had left his little bag behind. He turned back, but the train had gone away.

'Ah, there you are!' said the Porter. 'This way! What! No luggage? You will have to go to the Workhouse.'

Niggle felt very ill, and fainted on the platform. They put him in an ambulance and took him to the Workhouse Infirmary.

He did not like the treatment at all. The medicine they gave him was bitter. The officials and attendants were unfriendly, silent, and strict; and he never saw anyone else, except a very severe doctor, who visited him occasionally. It was more like being in a prison than in a hospital. He had to work hard, at stated hours: at digging, carpentry, and painting bare boards all one plain colour. He was never allowed outside, and the windows all looked inwards. They kept him in the dark for hours at a stretch, 'to do some thinking,' they said. He lost count of time. He did not even begin to feel better, not if that could be judged by whether he felt any pleasure in doing anything. He did not, not even in getting into bed.

At first, during the first century or so (I am merely giving his impressions), he used to worry aimlessly about the past. One thing he kept on repeating to himself, as he lay in the dark: 'I wish I had called on Parish the first morning after the high winds began. I meant to. The first loose tiles would have been easy to fix. Then Mrs Parish might never have caught cold. Then I should not have caught cold either. Then I should have had a week longer.' But in time he forgot what it was that he had wanted a week longer for. If he worried at all after that, it was about his jobs in the hospital. He planned them out, thinking how quickly he could stop that board creaking, or rehang that door, or mend that table-leg. Probably he really became rather useful, though no one ever told him so. But that, of course, cannot have been the reason why they kept the poor little man so long. They may have been waiting for him to get better, and judging 'better' by some odd medical standard of their own.

At any rate, poor Niggle got no pleasure out of

life, not what he had been used to call pleasure. He was certainly not amused. But it could not be denied that he began to have a feeling of – well satisfaction: bread rather than jam. He could take up a task the moment one bell rang, and lay it aside promptly the moment the next one went, all tidy and ready to be continued at the right time. He got through quite a lot in a day, now; he finished small things off neatly. He had no 'time of his own' (except alone in his bed-cell), and yet he was becoming master of his time; he began to know just what he could do with it. There was no sense of rush. He was quieter inside now, and at resting-time he could really rest.

Then suddenly they changed all his hours; they hardly let him go to bed at all; they took him off carpentry altogether and kept him at plain digging, day after day. He took it fairly well. It was a long while before he even began to grope in the back of his mind for the curses that he had practically forgotten. He went on digging, till his back seemed broken, his hands were raw, and he felt that he could not manage another spadeful. Nobody thanked him. But the doctor came and looked at him.

'Knock off!' he said. 'Complete rest – in the dark.'

Niggle was lying in the dark, resting completely; so that, as he had not been either feeling or thinking at all, he might have been lying there for hours or for years, as far as he could tell. But now he heard Voices: not voices that he had ever heard before. There seemed to be a Medical Board, or perhaps a Court of Inquiry, going on close at hand, in an adjoining room with the door open, possibly, though he could not see any light.

'Now the Niggle case,' said a Voice, a severe voice, more severe than the doctor's.

'What was the matter with him?' said a Second Voice, a voice that you might have called gentle, though it was not soft – it was a voice of authority, and sounded at once hopeful and sad. 'What was the matter with Niggle? His heart was in the right place.'

'Yes, but it did not function properly,' said the First Voice. 'And his head was not screwed on tight enough: he hardly ever thought at all. Look at the time he wasted, not even amusing himself! He never got ready for his journey. He was moderately well-off, and yet he arrived here almost destitute, and had to be put in the paupers' wing. A bad case, I am afraid. I think he should stay some time yet.'

'It would not do him any harm, perhaps,' said the Second Voice. 'But, of course, he is only a little man. He was never meant to be anything very much; and he was never very strong. Let us look at the Records. Yes. There are some favourable points, you know.'

'Perhaps,' said the First Voice; 'but very few that will really bear examination.'

'Well,' said the Second Voice, 'there are these. He was a painter by nature. In a minor way, of course; still, a Leaf by Niggle has a charm of its own. He took a great deal of pains with leaves, just for their own sake. But he never thought that that made him important. There is no note in the Records of his pretending, even to himself, that it excused his neglect of things ordered by the law.'

'Then he should not have neglected so many,' said the First Voice.

'All the same, he did answer a good many Calls.'

'A small percentage, mostly of the easier sort, and he called those Interruptions. The Records are full of the word, together with a lot of complaints and silly imprecations.'

'True; but they looked like interruptions to him, of course, poor little man. And there is this: he never expected any Return, as so many of his sort call it. There is the Parish case, the one that came in later. He was Niggle's neighbour, never did a stroke for him, and seldom showed any gratitude at all. But there is no note in the Records that Niggle expected Parish's gratitude; he does not seem to have thought about it.'

'Yes, that is a point,' said the First Voice; 'but rather small. I think you will find Niggle often merely forgot. Things he had to do for Parish he put out of his mind as a nuisance he had done with.'

'Still, there is this last report,' said the Second Voice, 'that wet bicycle-ride. I rather lay stress on that. It seems plain that this was a genuine sacrifice: Niggle guessed that he was throwing away his last chance with his picture, and he guessed, too, that Parish was worrying unnecessarily.'

'I think you put it too strongly,' said the First Voice. 'But you have the last word. It is your task, of course, to put the best interpretation on the facts. Sometimes they will bear it. What do you propose?'

'I think it is a case for a little gentle treatment now,' said the Second Voice.

Niggle thought that he had never heard anything so generous as that Voice. It made Gentle Treatment sound like a load of rich gifts, and a summons to a King's feast. Then suddenly Niggle felt ashamed. To hear that he was considered a case for Gentle Treatment overwhelmed him, and made him blush in the dark. It was like being publicly praised, when you and all the audience knew that the praise was not deserved. Niggle hid his blushes in the rough blanket.

There was a silence. Then the First Voice spoke to Niggle, quite close. 'You have been listening,' it said.

'Yes,' said Niggle.

'Well, what have you to say?'

'Could you tell me about Parish?' said Niggle. 'I should like to see him again. I hope he is not very ill? Can you cure his leg? It used to give him a wretched time. And please don't worry about him and me. He was a very good neighbour, and let me have excellent potatoes, very cheap, which saved me a lot of time.'

'Did he?' said the First Voice. 'I am glad to hear it.'

There was another silence. Niggle heard the

Voices receding. 'Well, I agree,' he heard the First Voice say in the distance. 'Let him go on to the next stage. Tomorrow, if you like.'

Niggle woke up to find that his blinds were drawn, and his little cell was full of sunshine. He got up, and found that some comfortable clothes had been put out for him, not hospital uniform. After breakfast the doctor treated his sore hands, putting some salve on them that healed them at once. He gave Niggle some good advice, and a bottle of tonic (in case he needed it). In the middle of the morning they gave Niggle a biscuit and a glass of wine; and then they gave him a ticket.

'You can go to the railway station now,' said the doctor. 'The Porter will look after you. Goodbye.'

Niggle slipped out of the main door, and blinked a little. The sun was very bright. Also he had expected to walk out into a large town, to match the size of the station; but he did not. He was on the top of a hill, green, bare, swept by a keen invigorating wind. Nobody else was about. Away down under the hill he could see the roof of the station shining.

He walked downhill to the station briskly, but without hurry. The Porter spotted him at once.

'This way!' he said, and led Niggle to a bay, in which there was a very pleasant little local train standing: one coach, and a small engine, both very bright, clean, and newly painted. It looked as if this was their first run. Even the track that lay in front of the engine looked new: the rails shone, the chairs were painted green, and the sleepers gave off a delicious smell of fresh tar in the warm sunshine. The coach was empty.

'Where does this train go, Porter?' asked Niggle.

'I don't think they have fixed its name yet,' said the Porter. 'But you'll find it all right.' He shut the door.

The train moved off at once. Niggle lay back in his seat. The little engine puffed along in a deep cutting with high green banks, roofed with blue sky. It did not seem very long before the engine gave a whistle, the brakes were put on, and the train stopped. There was no station, and no signboard, only a flight of steps up the green embankment. At the top of the steps there was a wicket-gate in a trim hedge. By the gate stood his bicycle; at least, it looked like his, and there was a yellow label tied to the bars with NIGGLE written on it in large black letters.

Niggle pushed open the gate, jumped on the bicycle, and went bowling downhill in the spring sunshine. Before long he found that the path on which he had started had disappeared, and the bicycle was rolling along over a marvellous turf. It was green and close; and yet he could see every blade distinctly. He seemed to remember having seen or dreamed of that sweep of grass somewhere or other. The curves of the land were familiar somehow. Yes: the ground was becoming level, as it should, and now, of course, it was beginning to rise again. A great green shadow came between him and the sun. Niggle looked up, and fell off his bicycle.

Before him stood the Tree, his Tree, finished. If you could say that of a Tree that was alive, its leaves opening, its branches growing and bending in the wind that Niggle had so often felt or guessed, and had so often failed to catch. He gazed at the Tree, and slowly he lifted his arms and opened them wide.

'It's a gift!' he said. He was referring to his art, and also to the result; but he was using the word quite literally.

He went on looking at the Tree. All the leaves he had ever laboured at were there, as he had imagined them rather than as he had made them; and there were others that had only budded in his mind, and many that might have budded, if only he had had time. Nothing was written on them, they were just exquisite leaves, yet they were dated as clear as a calendar. Some of the most beautiful – and the most characteristic, the most perfect examples of the Niggle style – were seen to have been produced in collaboration with Mr Parish: there was no other way of putting it.

The birds were building in the Tree. Astonishing birds: how they sang! They were mating, hatching, growing wings, and flying away singing into the Forest even while he looked at them. For now he saw that the Forest was there too, opening out on either side, and marching away into the distance. The Mountains were glimmering far away.

After a time Niggle turned towards the Forest. Not because he was tired of the Tree, but he seemed to have got it all clear in his mind now, and was aware of it, and of its growth, even when he was not looking at it. As he walked away, he discovered an odd thing: the Forest, of course, was a distant

Forest, yet he could approach it, even enter it, without its losing that particular charm. He had never before been able to walk into the distance without turning it into mere surroundings. It really added a considerable attraction to walking in the country, because, as you walked, new distances opened out; so that you now had double, treble, and quadruple distances, doubly, trebly, and quadruply enchanting. You could go on and on, and have a whole country in a garden, or in a picture (if you preferred to call it that). You could go on and on, but not perhaps for ever. There were the Mountains in the background. They did get nearer, very slowly. They did not seem to belong to the picture, or only as a link to something else, a glimpse through the trees of something different, a further stage: another picture.

Niggle walked about, but he was not merely pottering. He was looking round carefully. The Tree was finished, though not finished with – 'Just the other way about to what it used to be,' he thought – but in the Forest there were a number of inconclusive regions, that still needed work and thought. Nothing needed altering any longer, nothing was wrong, as far as it had gone, but it needed continuing up to a definite point. Niggle saw the point precisely, in each case.

He sat down under a very beautiful distant tree – a variation of the Great Tree, but quite individual, or it would be with a little more attention – and he considered where to begin work, and where to end it, and how much time was required. He could not quite work out his scheme.

'Of course!' he said. 'What I need is Parish. There are lots of things about earth, plants, and trees that he knows and I don't. This place cannot be left just as my private park. I need help and advice: I ought to have got it sooner.'

He got up and walked to the place where he had decided to begin work. He took off his coat. Then, down in a little sheltered hollow hidden from a further view, he saw a man looking round rather bewildered. He was leaning on a spade, but plainly did not know what to do. Niggle hailed him. 'Parish!' he called.

Parish shouldered his spade and came up to him. He still limped a little. They did not speak, just nodded as they used to do, passing in the lane, but now they walked about together, arm in arm. Without talking, Niggle and Parish agreed exactly where to make the small house and garden, which seemed to be required.

As they worked together, it became plain that Niggle was now the better of the two at ordering his time and getting things done. Oddly enough, it was Niggle who became most absorbed in building and gardening, while Parish often wondered about looking at trees, and especially at the Tree.

One day Niggle was busy planting a quickset hedge, and Parish was lying on the grass near by, looking attentively at a beautiful and shapely little yellow flower growing in the green turf. Niggle had put a lot of them among the roots of his Tree long ago. Suddenly parish looked up: his face was glistening in the sun, and he was smiling.

'This is grand!' he said. 'I oughtn't to be here, really. Thank you for putting in a word for me.'

'Nonsense,' said Niggle. 'I don't remember what I said, but anyway it was not nearly enough.'

'Oh yes, it was,' said Parish. 'It got me out a lot sooner. That Second Voice, you know: he had me sent here; he said you had asked to see me. I owe it to you.'

'No. You owe it to the Second Voice,' said Niggle. 'We both do.'

They went on living and working together: I do not know how long. It is no use denying that at first they occasionally disagreed, especially when they got tired. For at first they did sometimes get tired. They found that they had both been provided with tonics. Each bottle had the same label: *A few drops to be taken in water from the Spring, before resting.*

They found the Spring in the heart of the Forest; only once long ago had Niggle imagined it, but he had never drawn it. Now he perceived that it was the source of the lake that glimmered, far away and the nourishment of all that grew in the country. The few drops made the water astringent, rather bitter, but invigorating; and it cleared the head. After drinking they rested alone; and then they got up again and things went on merrily. At such times Niggle would think of wonderful new flowers and plants, and Parish always knew exactly how to set them and where they would do best. Long before the tonics were finished they had ceased to need them. Parish lost his limp.

As their work drew to an end they allowed themselves more and more time for walking about, looking at the trees, and the flowers, and the lights and shapes, and the lie of the land. Sometimes they sang together; but Niggle found that he was now beginning to turn his eyes, more and more often, towards the Mountains.

The time came when the house in the hollow, the garden, the grass, the forest, the lake, and all the country was nearly complete, in its own proper fashion. The Great Tree was in full blossom.

'We shall finish this evening,' said Parish one day. 'After that we will go for a really long walk.'

They set out next day, and they walked until they came right through the distances to the Edge. It was not visible, of course: there was no line, or fence, or wall; but they knew that they had come to the margin of that country. They saw a man, he looked like a shepherd; he was walking towards them, down the grass-slopes that led up into the Mountains.

'Do you want a guide?' he asked. 'Do you want to go on?'

For a moment a shadow fell between Niggle and Parish, for Niggle knew that he did now want to go on, and (in a sense) ought to go on; but Parish did not want to go on, and was not yet ready to go.

'I must wait for my wife,' said Parish to Niggle. 'She'd be lonely. I rather gathered that they would send her after me, some time or other, when she was ready, and when I had got things ready for her. The house is finished now, as well as we could make it; but I should like to show it to her. She'll be able to make it better, I expect: more homely. I hope she'll like this country, too.' He turned to the shepherd. 'Are you a guide?' he asked. 'Could you tell me the name of this country?'

'Don't you know?' said the man. 'It is Niggle's Country. It is Niggle's Picture, or most of it: a little of it is now Parish's Garden.'

'Niggle's Picture!' said Parish in astonishment. 'Did *you* think of all this, Niggle? I never knew you were so clever. Why didn't you tell me?'

'He tried to tell you long ago,' said the man, 'but you would not look. He had only got canvas and paint in those days, and you wanted to mend your roof with them. This is what you and your wife used to call Niggle's Nonsense, or That Daubing.'

'But it did not look like this then, not *real*,' said Parish.

'No, it was only a glimpse then,' said the man; 'but you might have caught the glimpse, if you had ever thought it worth while to try.'

'I did not give you much chance,' said Niggle. 'I never tried to explain. I used to call you Old

Earth-grubber. But what does it matter? We have lived and worked together now. Things might have been different, but they could not have been better. All the same, I am afraid I shall have to be going on. We shall meet again, I expect: there must be many more things we can do together. Goodbye!' He shook Parish's hand warmly: a good, firm, honest hand it seemed. He turned and looked back for a moment. The blossom on the Great Tree was shining like flame. All the birds were flying in the air and singing. Then he smiled and nodded to Parish and went off with the shepherd.

He was going to learn about sheep, and the high pasturages, and look at a wider sky, and walk ever further and further towards the Mountains, always uphill. Beyond that I cannot guess what became of him. Even little Niggle in his old home could glimpse the Mountains far away, and they got into the borders of his picture; but what they are really like, and what lies beyond them only those can say who have climbed them.

'I think he was a silly little man,' said Councillor Tompkins. 'Worthless, in fact; no use to Society at all.'

'Oh, I don't know,' said Atkins, who was nobody of importance, just a schoolmaster. 'I am not so sure; it depends on what you mean by use.'

'No practical or economic use,' said Tompkins. 'I dare say he could have been made into a serviceable cog of some sort, if you schoolmasters knew your business. But you don't, and so we get useless people of his sort. If I ran this country I should put him and his like to some job that they're fit for, washing dishes in a communal kitchen or something, and I should see that they did it properly. Or I would put them away. I should have put *him* away long ago.'

'Put him away? You mean you'd have made him start on the journey before his time?'

'Yes, if you must use that meaningless old expression. Push him through the tunnel into the great Rubbish Heap: that's what I mean.'

'Then you don't think painting is worth anything, not worth preserving, or improving, or even making use of?'

'Of course, painting has uses,' said Tompkins. 'But you couldn't make use of his painting. There is plenty of scope for bold young men not afraid of new ideas and new methods. None for this

40

old-fashioned stuff. Private daydreaming. He could not have designed a telling poster to save his life. Always fiddling with leaves and flowers. I asked him why, once. He said he thought they were pretty! Can you believe it? He said *pretty*! "What, digestive and genital organs of plants?" I said to him; and he had nothing to answer. Silly footler.'

'Footler,' sighed Atkins. 'Yes, poor little man, he never finished anything. Ah well, his canvases have been put to "better uses", since he went. But I am not so sure, Tompkins. You remember that large one, the one they used to patch the damaged house next door to his, after the gales and floods? I found a corner of it torn off, lying in a field. It was damaged, but legible: a mountain-peak and a spray of leaves. I can't get it out of my mind.'

'Out of your what?' said Tompkins.

'Who are you two talking about?' said Perkins, intervening in the cause of peace: Atkins had flushed rather red.

'The name's not worth repeating,' said Tompkins. 'I don't know why we are talking about him at all. He did not live in town.'

'No,' said Atkins; 'but you had your eye on his house, all the same. That is why you used to go and call, and sneer at him while drinking his tea. Well, you've got his house now, as well as the one in town, so you need not grudge him his name. We were talking about Niggle, if you want to know, Perkins.'

'Oh, poor little Niggle!' said Perkins. 'Never knew he painted.'

That was probably the last time Niggle's name ever came up in conversation. However, Atkins preserved the odd corner. Most of it crumbled; but one beautiful leaf remained intact. Atkins had it framed. Later he left it to the Town Museum, and for a long time while 'Leaf: by Niggle' hung there in a recess, and was noticed by a few eyes. But eventually the Museum was burnt down, and the leaf, and Niggle, were entirely forgotten in his old country.

'It is proving very useful indeed,' said the Second Voice. 'As a holiday, and a refreshment. It is splendid for convalescence; and not only for that, for many it is the best introduction to the Mountains. It works wonders in some cases. I am sending more and more there. They seldom have to come back.'

'No, that is so,' said the First Voice. 'I think we shall have to give the region a name. What do you propose?'

'The Porter settled that some time ago,' said the Second Voice. '*Train for Niggle's Parish in the bay*: he has shouted that for a long while now. Niggle's Parish. I sent a message to both of them to tell them.'

'What did they say?'

'They both laughed. Laughed – the Mountains rang with it!'

AFTERWORD

BY
Tom Shippey

'FAËRIE is a perilous land, and in it are pit-falls for the unwary and dungeons for the overbold ... The realm of fairy-story is wide and deep and high and filled with many things: all manner of beasts and birds are found there; shoreless seas and stars uncounted; beauty that is an enchantment, and an ever-present peril; both joy and sorrow as sharp as swords. In that realm a man may, perhaps, count himself fortunate to have wandered, but its very richness and strangeness tie the tongue of a traveller who would report them. And while he is there it is dangerous for him to ask too many questions, lest the gates should be shut and the keys be lost.'

J.R.R. Tolkien[1]

[1] From *On Fairy-stories*, a lecture given on 8 March 1939.

WE DO NOT KNOW when Tolkien began to turn his thoughts to the Perilous Realm of Faërie. In his essay 'On Fairy-stories', he admits that he took no particular interest in tales of that kind as a child: they were just one of many interests. A 'real taste' for them, he says, 'was wakened by philology on the threshold of manhood, and quickened to full life by war'. This seems to be strictly accurate. The first of his works to take an interest in fairies, that we know of, is a poem called 'Wood-sunshine', written in 1910, when Tolkien was eighteen and still at King Edward's School in Birmingham. By the end of 1915, the year in which he took his Oxford degree and immediately joined the army to fight in the Great War, he had written several more, some of them containing major elements of what would be his developed Faërie mythology. By the end of 1917, most of which he spent in military hospital or wait-ing to be passed fit for active service once more, he had written the first draft of tales which would sixty years later be published in *The Silmarillion*, and much of Middle-earth, as also of Elvenhome beyond it, had taken shape in his mind.

What happened then is a long story, about which we now know a great deal more than we did, but once again it was summed up concisely and suggestively by Tolkien himself, in the story 'Leaf by Niggle'. It is generally accepted that this has a strong element of self-portrait about it, with Tolkien the writer – a confirmed 'niggler', as he said himself – transposed as Niggle the painter. Niggle, the story tells us, was busy on all kinds of pictures, but one in particular started to grow on him. It began as just a single leaf, but then it became a tree, and the tree grew to be a Tree, and behind it a whole country started to open out, with 'glimpses of a forest marching over the land, and of mountains tipped with snow'. Niggle, Tolkien wrote, 'lost interest in his other pictures; or else he took them and tacked them on to the edges of his great picture'.

Once again this is an accurate account of what Tolkien can be seen doing in the 1920s, 1930s, and 1940s. During those thirty years he kept working at variants of 'Silmarillion' stories, writing occasional poems, often anonymously, and making up other stories, not always written down and sometimes told initially only to his children. *The Hobbit* started life as one of these, set in Middle-earth, but to begin with connected only tangentially with the Elvish history of the Silmarils: it was, to use the modern term, a spin-off. *The Lord of the Rings* was a further spin-off, this time from *The Hobbit*, and initially motivated by Tolkien's publisher's strong desire for a *Hobbit*-sequel. But what Tolkien started to do, just like Niggle, was to take things he had written before and start 'tacking them on to the edges'. Tom Bombadil, who had begun as the name for a child's toy, got into print in 1934 as the hero of a poem, and then became perhaps the most mysterious figure in the world of *The Lord of the Rings*. That work also drew in other poems, some of them comic, like Sam Gamgee's 'Oliphaunt' rhyme, first published in 1927, others grave and sad, like the version Strider gives on Weathertop of the tale of Beren and Lúthien, again going back to a poem published in 1925, and based on a story written even earlier.

Quite what was the 'leaf' of Tolkien's original inspiration, and what he meant by 'the Tree', we cannot be sure, though the 'forest marching over the land' does sound very like the Ents. But the little allegory makes one further point which corroborates what Tolkien said elsewhere, and that is that 'fairy-stories', whoever tells them, are not about fairies so much as about Faërie, the Perilous Realm itself. Tolkien indeed asserted there are not many stories actually *about* fairies, or even about elves, and most of them – he was too modest to add, unless they were written by Tolkien himself – were not very interesting. Most good fairy-stories are about 'the *aventures* of men in the Perilous Realm or upon its shadowy marches', a very exact description once again of Tolkien's own tales of Beren on the marches or borders of Doriath, Túrin skirmishing around Nargothrond, or Tuor escaping from the Fall of Gondolin. Tolkien remained strongly ambivalent about the very notion of 'fairy'. He disliked the word, as a borrowing from French – the English word is 'elf' – and he also disliked the whole Victorian cult of fairies as little, pretty, ineffective creatures, prone to being co-opted into the service of moral tales for children, and often irretrievably phony. Much of his essay 'On Fairy-stories', indeed (published in 1945 in a memorial volume for Charles Williams, and there expanded from a lecture given in 1939 in honour of Andrew Lang the fairy-tale collector) is avowedly corrective, both of scholarly terminology and of popular taste. Tolkien thought he knew better, was in touch with older, deeper, and more powerful conceptions than the Victorians knew, even those as learned as Andrew Lang.

However, while he had no time for fairies, Tolkien was all for Faërie itself, the land, as Bilbo Baggins puts it, of 'dragons and goblins and giants', the land where one may hear of 'the rescue of princesses and the unexpected luck of widow's sons'. The books *Roverandom*, *Farmer Giles of Ham*, *The Adventures of Tom Bombadil* and *Smith of Wootton Major* show Tolkien trying out various approaches to perilous realms of one kind or another, all of them suggestive, original, independent. They represent, one may say, the pictures Niggle did *not* 'tack on to the edges of his great picture'. They hint tantalisingly at directions which might have been explored further, like the later unwritten history of Farmer Giles's Little Kingdom. And they give quite different views of Tolkien's inspiration, spread over a period of at least forty years, and extending from maturity to old age. Also, as it happens, we know a good deal about how each of them came into being.

In 'Leaf by Niggle' Tolkien presents his vision of a world elsewhere, one with room in it for Middle-earth and Faërie and all other hearts' desires as well. Nevertheless, although it presents a 'divine comedy' and ends with world-shaking laughter, the story began in fear. Tolkien reported in more than one letter that the whole story came to him in a dream and that he wrote it down immediately, at some time (reports vary) between 1939 and 1942. This is the more plausible in that it is so obvious what kind of a dream it was: an anxiety dream, of the kind we all get. Students with an exam to take dream that they have overslept and missed it, academics due to make a presentation dream they have arrived on the podium with nothing to read and nothing in their heads, and the fear at the heart of 'Leaf by Niggle' is clearly that of *never getting finished*. Niggle knows he has a deadline – it is obviously death, the journey we all have to take – he has a painting he desperately wants to finish, but he puts things off and puts things off, and when he finally buckles down to it, first there is a call on his time he cannot refuse, and then he gets sick, and then an Inspector turns up and condemns his painting as scrap, and as he starts to contest this the

Driver turns up and tells him he must leave now with no more than he can snatch up. He leaves even that little bag on the train, and when he turns back for it, the train has gone. This kind of one-thing-after-another dream is all too familiar. The motive for it is also easy to imagine, in Tolkien's case. By 1940 he had been working on his 'Silmarillion' mythology for more than twenty years, and none of it had been published except for a scattering of poems and the 'spin-off' *The Hobbit*. He had been writing *The Lord of the Rings* since Christmas 1937, and it too was going slowly. His study was full of drafts and revisions. One can guess also that, like most professors, he found his many administrative duties a distraction, though Niggle (and perhaps Tolkien) is guiltily aware that he is easily distracted, and not a good manager of his time.

Concentration and time-management are what Niggle has to learn in the Workhouse, which most critics have identified as a version of Purgatory. His reward is to find that in the Other World, dreams come true: there before him is his Tree, better than he had ever painted it and better even than he had imagined it, and beyond it the Forest and the Mountains that he had only begun to imagine. And yet there is room for more improvement, and to make it Niggle has to work with his neighbour Parish, who in the real world had seemed only another distraction. What becomes their joint vision is recognized as therapeutically valuable even by the Voices who judge people's lives, but even then it is only an introduction to a greater vision mortals can only guess at. But everyone has to start somewhere. As the Fairy Queen says in *Smith of Wootton Major*, 'Better a little doll, maybe, than no memory of Faery at all', and better Faery than no sense of anything beyond the mundane world of everyday.

'Leaf' after all has two endings, one in the Other World and one in the world which Niggle left. The Other World ending is one of joy and laughter, but in the real world hope and memory are crushed. Niggle's great painting of the Tree was used to patch a hole, one leaf of it went to a museum, but that too was burned down and Niggle was entirely forgotten. The last words ever said about him are 'never knew he painted', and the future seems to belong to people like Councillor Tompkins, with his views on practical education and – remember that this is a story of at latest the early 1940s – the elimination of undesirable elements of Society. If there is a remedy for us, Tolkien says, stressing that Niggle uses the word 'quite literally', it will be 'a gift'. Another word for 'gift' is 'grace'.

'Leaf by Niggle' ends, then, both with what Tolkien in 'On Fairy-stories' calls 'dyscatastrophe ... sorrow and failure', and with what he regards as the 'highest function' of fairy-story and of *evangelium*, the 'good news' or Gospel beyond it, and that is 'eucatastrophe', the 'sudden joyous "turn"', the 'sudden and miraculous grace', which one finds in Grimm, in modern fairy-tale, and supremely in Tolkien's own 'Tales from the Perilous Realm'. In the Middle English poem *Sir Orfeo*, which Tolkien edited in 1943–4 (in an anonymous pamphlet of which, characteristically, hardly any copies survive), the barons comfort the steward who has just been told his lord is dead, 'and telleth him hou it geth, / It is no bot of mannes deth'. That's the way it goes, they say, there's no help for it, or as Tolkien rendered the last line in his posthumously-published translation of 1975, 'death of man no man can mend'. The barons are compassionate, well-intentioned, and above all sensible: that *is* the way things go. But the poem proves them wrong, just this once, for Orfeo is alive, and has rescued his queen from captivity in

Faërie as well. We find the same 'turn' in *The Lord of the Rings*, as Sam, who has lain down to die on Mount Doom after the destruction of the Ring, wakes to find himself alive, rescued, and faced by the resurrected Gandalf. There is joy in the Perilous Realm, and on its Dark Marches too, all the stronger for the real-life sorrows and losses which it challenges and surmounts.

TOM SHIPPEY

OF FURTHER INTEREST

Roverandom

While on holiday in 1925, four-year-old Michael Tolkien lost his beloved toy dog on the beach. To console him, his father, J.R.R. Tolkien, improvised a story about Rover, a real dog who is magically transformed into a toy, and his quest to find the wizard who can return him to normal.

The adventures of Rover, or 'Roverandom' as he becomes known, include encounters with an ancient sand-sorcerer and a terrible dragon, by the king of the sea and the man-in-the moon. Rich in wit and wordplay, the story underwent a number of revisions and was originally considered for publication in January 1937, the same year as *The Hobbit*, but was abandoned when the publishers asked instead for a sequel, which culminated in *The Lord of the Rings*. *Roverandom* was finally published in 1998.

'This is an old-fashoned story, yet it still speaks freshly today . . . would leap to life when read aloud to a child.'
THE INDEPENDENT

Farmer Giles of Ham

Farmer Giles of Ham did not look like a hero. He was fat and read-bearded and enjoyed a slow, comfortable life. But after inadvertently scaring away a rather deaf and short-sighted giant, Farmer Giles' heroic reputation spread far and wide. Unfortunately for him, when the wily dragon Chrysophylax visited the kingdom, it was Farmer Giles who was called upon to do battle with it . . .

Like *The Hobbit* and *Roverandom*, *Farmer Giles of Ham* was invented by J.R.R. Tolkien at first to entertain his children, then grew and became more elaborate. Its final version is for readers of all ages who enjoy a good story told with wit and imagination.

'A fabulous tale of the days when giants and dragons walked the kingdom.' SUNDAY TIMES

The Adventures of
Tom Bombadil

'Here is something that no devotee of the Hobbit epic can afford to miss, while awaiting a further instalment of the history of these fascinating people.' So declared the jacket of this book when it was first published some fifty years ago.

One of the most intriguing characters in *The Lord of the Rings*, the amusing and enigmatic Tom Bombadil, also appears in verses said to have been written by Hobbits and preserved in the 'Red Book' with stories of Bilbo and Frodo Baggins and their friends. *The Adventures of Tom Bombadil* collects these and other poems, mainly concerned with legends and jests of the Shire at the end of the Third Age.

'*Professor Tolkien revealed in the verses scattered through* The Hobbit *that he had a talent for songs, riddling rhymes, and a kind of balladry. In* The Adventures of Tom Bombadil *the talent can be seen to be close to genius.*'   THE LISTENER

Smith of Wootton Major

Every 24 years in the village of Wootton Major, the Feast of Good Children was held. To celebrate it a Great Cake was prepared, to feed the 24 children who were invited. The cake was very sweet and rich and entirely covered in sugar icing. But inside there were some very strange ingredients and whoever swallowed one of them would gain the gift of entry into the Land of Faery . . .

What began as a preface to *The Golden Key* by George MacDonald eventually grew into this charming short story. Composed almost a decade after *The Lord of the Rings*, and when his lifelong occupation with creating *The Silmarillion* was winding down, *Smith of Wootton Major* was the product of ripened experience and reflection, and would be the last work of fiction to be published in Tolkien's own lifetime.

'The book has a haunting quality, characteristic of the best of the "deeper" folk tales. It is a beautiful, memorable story.' TIMES EDUCATIONAL SUPPLEMENT